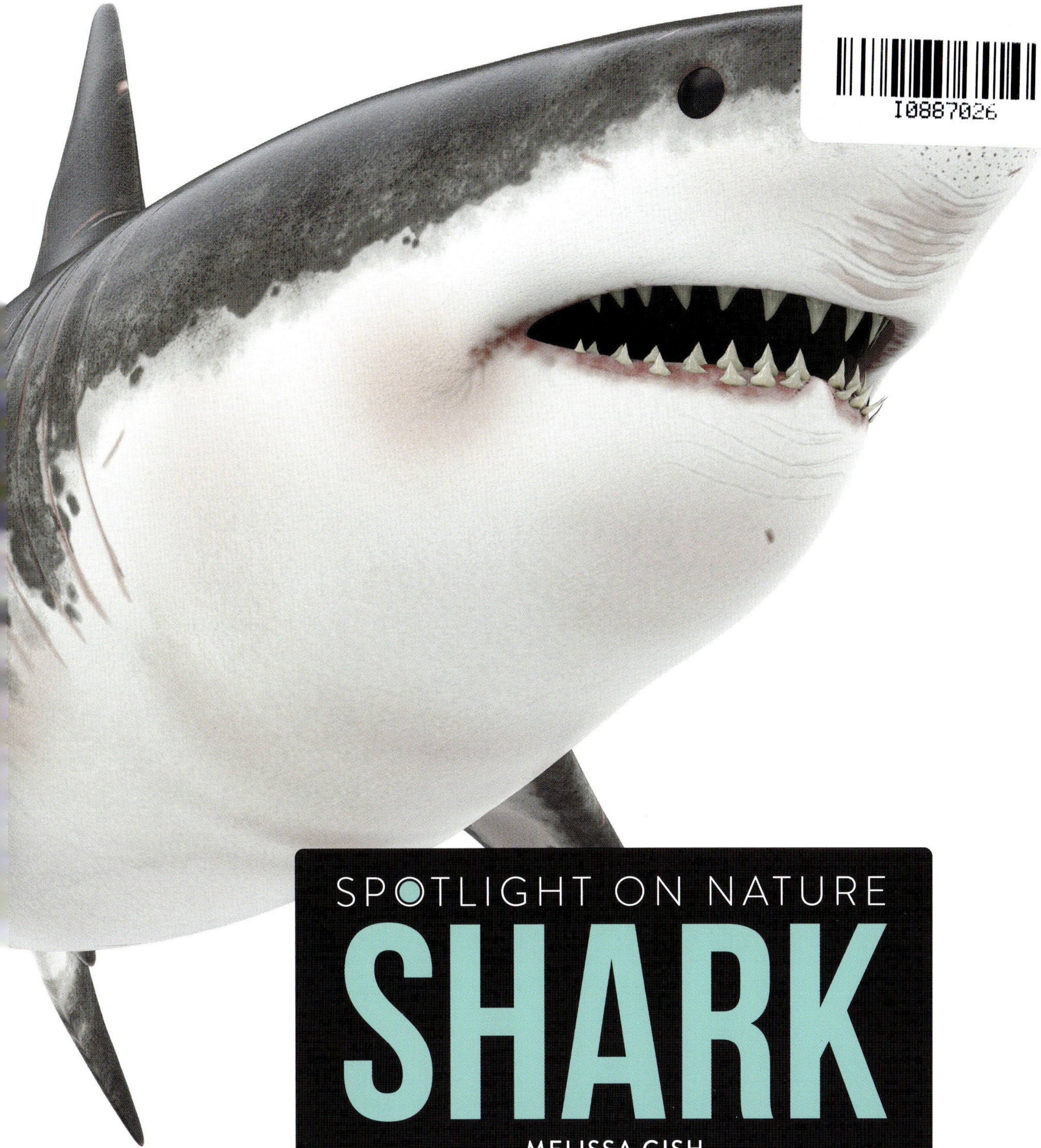

SPOTLIGHT ON NATURE

SHARK

MELISSA GISH

CREATIVE EDUCATION • CREATIVE PAPERBACKS

Published by Creative Education and Creative Paperbacks
P.O. Box 227, Mankato, Minnesota 56002
Creative Education and Creative Paperbacks are imprints
of The Creative Company
www.thecreativecompany.us

Design by Chelsey Luther; production by Colin O'Dea
Art direction by Rita Marshall
Printed in the United States of America

Photographs by Alamy (Kelvin Aitken, Danita Delimont, FLPA, imageBROKER, Nerthuz, Peter Pinnock, Scubazoo, Stephen Frink Collection, Stocktrek Images, Inc., WaterFrame, Wildestanimal), Dreamstime (Christopher Elwell), Getty Images (Rodrigo Friscione, Gregory S. Paulson/Cultura, Ryan Sault/EyeEm), iStockphoto (ARTYuSTUDIO, bearacreative, bennymarty, Dole08, NaluPhoto, Tolga TEZCAN, Michael Zeigler), Minden Pictures (Yves Lefevre/Biosphoto), National Geographic Creative (JENNIFER HAYES), Shutterstock (Stefan Pircher, Martin Prochazkacz, Seashell World)

Library of Congress Cataloging-in-Publication Data
Names: Gish, Melissa, author.
Title: Shark / Melissa Gish.
Series: Spotlight on nature.
Includes index.
Summary: A detailed chronology of developmental milestones drives this life study of sharks, including their habitats, physical features, and conservation measures taken to protect these cartilaginous fish.
Identifiers: ISBN 978-1-64026-344-4 (hardcover) / ISBN 978-1-62832-876-9 (pbk) / ISBN 978-1-64000-486-3 (eBook)
This title has been submitted for CIP processing under LCCN 2020902419.

First Edition HC 9 8 7 6 5 4 3 2 1
First Edition PBK 9 8 7 6 5 4 3 2 1

CONTENTS

MEET THE FAMILY

SCALLOPED HAMMERHEAD SHARKS

of Santa Cruz Island

The Galápagos Islands lie about 620 miles (998 km) off the coast of Ecuador. Santa Cruz Island is in the middle of Galápagos Marine Reserve. This is a protected area where fishing is limited and other human interference is not allowed. The waters of the reserve are rich with sea life that includes manta rays, moray eels, green sea turtles, and as many as 32 different shark **species**.

Off the western coast of Santa Cruz, a female scalloped hammerhead shark cruises over a colorful coral landscape toward a shallow lagoon. The lagoon is near a mangrove forest where the underwater tangle of roots provides shelter for young sea creatures. The shark reaches the lagoon's sandy seabed. She feels the warm summer sun on her back. For nearly 10 months, baby sharks have been growing inside her body. The hammerhead is about to give birth.

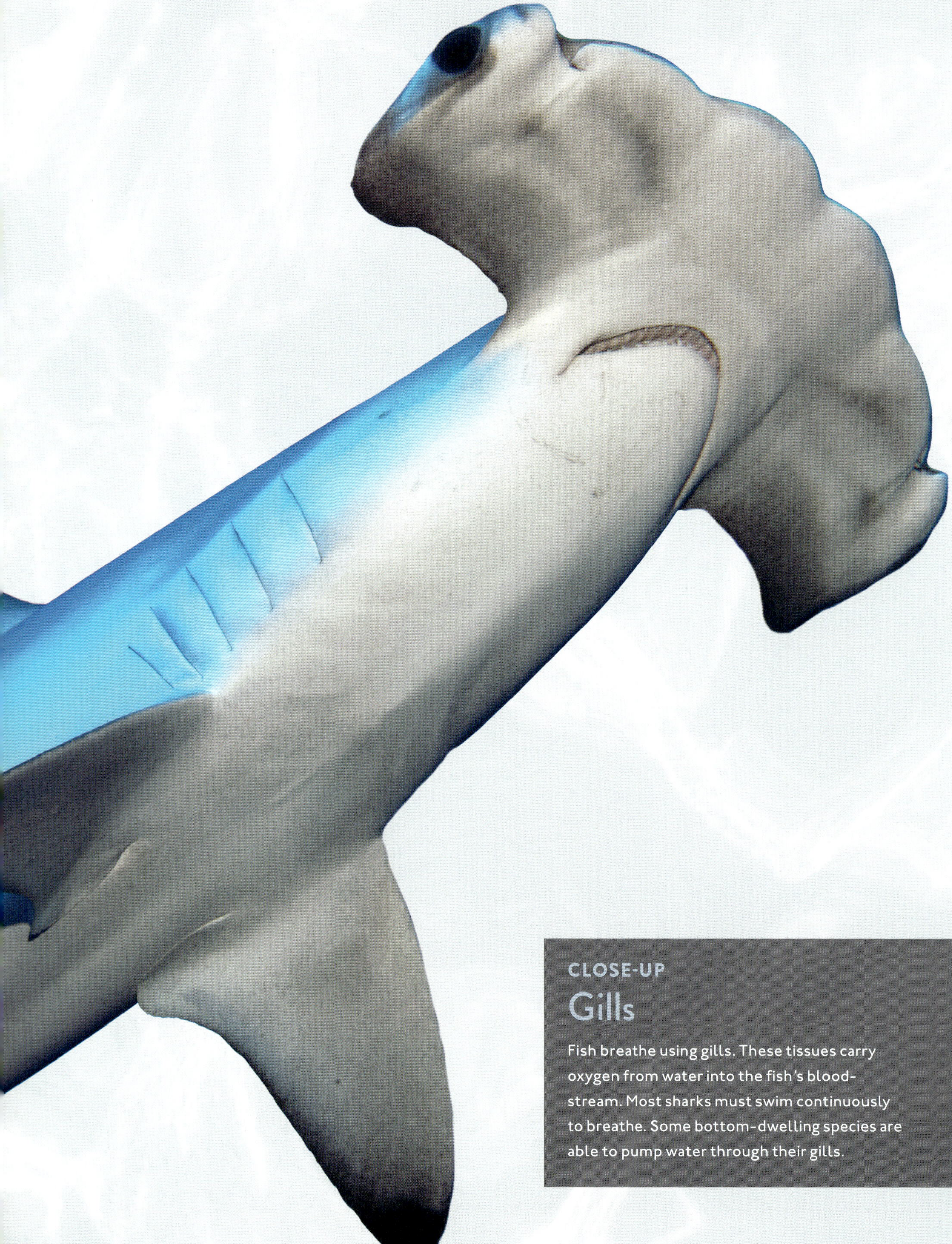

CLOSE-UP

Gills

Fish breathe using gills. These tissues carry oxygen from water into the fish's bloodstream. Most sharks must swim continuously to breathe. Some bottom-dwelling species are able to pump water through their gills.

CHAPTER ONE

LIFE BEGINS

Sharks and their relatives (rays, skates, and chimaeras) are unique among fish. Their skeletons are made of cartilage instead of bone. Around 500 different shark species have been discovered and named. Some large sharks, such as tiger, mako, great white, bull, and blue sharks, are apex predators. This means they are at the top of their food chains. They hunt other sea creatures and have no natural predators. The largest shark species—whale and basking sharks—are not hunters at all. They roam with their mouths open, filtering tiny organisms called plankton from the water. About 80 percent of all shark species grow to lengths of no more than five feet (1.5 m).

SANTA CRUZ SCALLOPED HAMMERHEAD SHARK MILESTONES

DAY 1

- Born
- Length: 15.5 inches (39.4 cm)
- Weight: 18 ounces (510 g)

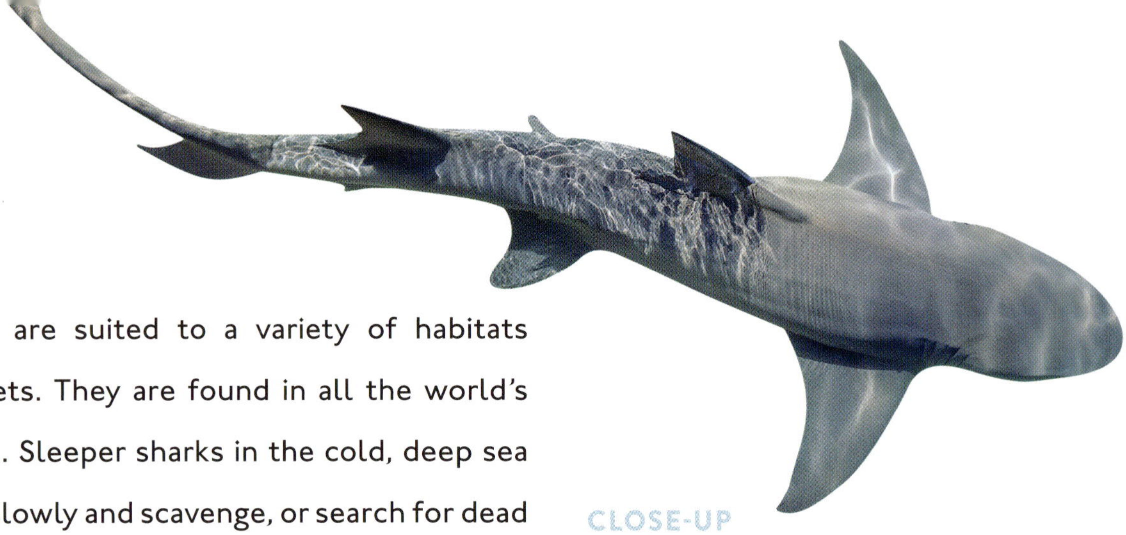

Sharks are suited to a variety of habitats and diets. They are found in all the world's oceans. Sleeper sharks in the cold, deep sea move slowly and scavenge, or search for dead animals to eat. Open-ocean species such as mako and salmon sharks are streamlined for speed so that they can chase down prey. Bottom-dwelling sharks typically have flat bodies. They lie hidden on the seabed and launch surprise attacks. Hammerheads use their broad heads, called cephalofoils, to pin rays and other prey to the seafloor before biting with relatively small jaws. Baby sharks, called pups, are equipped with teeth and the instincts to use them.

CLOSE-UP

Bendy bodies

Lightweight cartilage and no ribs enable sharks to swim quickly, turn sharply, and bend at sharp angles to capture prey. Their backbone and jaw cartilage hardens over time.

FEATURED FAMILY

Welcome to the World

The lagoon is about four feet (1.2 m) deep. The sun has warmed the water to 82 °F (27.8 °C). The scalloped hammerhead swims in slow circles, pushing pups out of her body one by one. Each is attached to an umbilical cord, which breaks, leaving a tiny wound in the pup's belly. In just a few minutes, 32 pups are born. As her mother swims back toward the sea, the last-born hammerhead darts into the tangle of mangrove roots.

Some sharks lay eggs, while others give birth to fully formed live young. About a third of shark species hatch from egg cases lain among rocks or beds of seagrass. Others hatch from eggs inside their mother's body and continue to grow until they are ready to be born. Still others are born after growing in fluid-filled sacs in their mother's body. Like most fish, sharks do not take care of their young. Great whites usually have 2 to 12 babies. The five-foot-long (1.5 m) offspring can fend for themselves. Smaller pups find survival more challenging. To compensate for big losses, some shark species have big litters. Tiger sharks, for example, have up to 80 pups at a time.

(3) WEEKS

- Wound from umbilical cord heals
- Length: 16.5 inches (41.9 cm)
- Weight: 20 ounces (567 g)

(6) MONTHS

- Feeds on larger crustaceans
- Length: 2 feet (0.6 m)
- Weight: 2 pounds (0.9 kg)

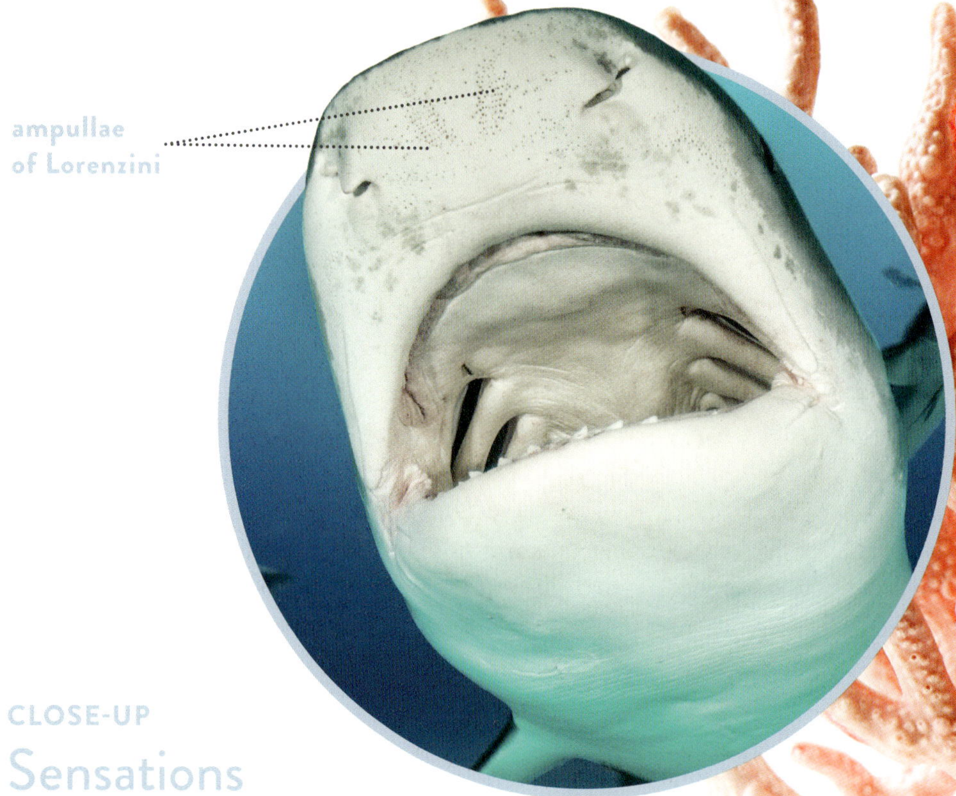

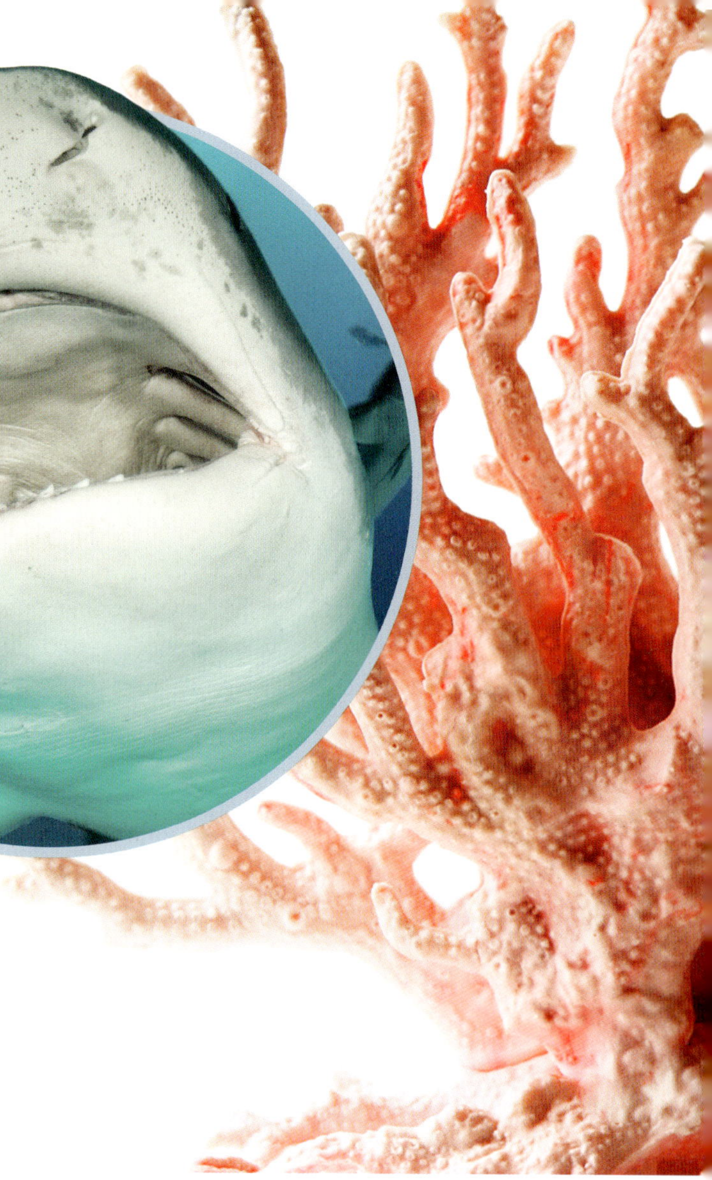

CLOSE-UP

Sensations

The pits on a shark's face are called ampullae of Lorenzini, and marks running from the snout to the tail are called lateral lines. These sense organs detect electrical energy and vibrations created by other living things in the water.

FEATURED FAMILY

First Meal

When the pup was in her mother's body, food came through the umbilical cord. Now she must find food on her own. Instinctively, she swims close to the seabed. Her senses tell her that something is moving beneath the sand. She touches the seabed with her forehead. A tiny crab scampers out, but the hammerhead is fast. She sucks the crab into her mouth, swallowing it whole. Then she glimpses several siblings biting at a patch of algae and rushes to join them.

Great whites USUALLY have 2 to 12 BABIES.

(18) MONTHS

- Experiences hunting challenges
- Length: 2.5 feet (0.8 m)
- Weight: 2.8 pounds (1.3 kg)

CLOSE-UP

Denticles

Sharkskin is covered with denticles. Each projection is actually a modified tooth! Denticles grow in tight layers with their tips pointing backward. Rubbing the skin from nose to tail feels smooth. Going the other direction can cause scrapes and cuts.

CHAPTER TWO

EARLY ADVENTURES

As youngsters, sharks typically eat anything they can find, from algae to dead animals. Or they eat anything they can catch. The more they eat, the faster they grow. Many pups die of starvation where food is scarce. And bigger sharks are a constant threat. Sharks that survive to adulthood can afford to be fussy eaters. Large, predatory sharks seek out fatty foods such as seals, sea lions, and baby whales. A great white shark can load up on food, digest it slowly, and not need to hunt again for several days or weeks. Fast-moving sharks burn more energy and must eat more often. To remain healthy, makos must consume 3 percent of their body weight in food every one or two days. They race after tuna, porpoises, and smaller sharks.

2.5 YEARS

- Leaves nursery lagoon
- Chased by tiger shark
- Length: 3 feet (0.9 m)

4 YEARS

- Settles on reef
- Hunting skills improve
- Length: 3.5 feet (1.1 m)
- Weight: 72 pounds (32.7 kg)

CLOSE-UP

Helpful fins

Side pectoral fins help a shark steer. Pelvic fins on the underside keep it from rolling over. The caudal fin, or tail, propels the shark forward. One or two dorsal fins on the back provide balance. Some species have an anal fin beneath the tail for added stability.

FEATURED FAMILY

Look Who's Learning

The little scalloped hammerhead is now one year old. She weaves among the mangrove roots, scouring the shadows for the juvenile sea bass and snappers that she can sense are hiding there. Suddenly, she feels huge vibrations and turns to investigate. An adult scalloped hammerhead swims into the lagoon. The young hammerhead watches as the older shark gives birth. When the shark leaves the lagoon, the young hammerhead's curiosity drives her from her hiding spot. The new pups flee as she approaches. She follows them, her brain processing their vibrations as they move. After a few moments, she turns away. They are far too large to consider eating.

Despite having a mouth full of teeth, sharks do not chew their food. If prey is too large to swallow, it will be broken off in chunks first. Many species do this by shaking their heads from side to side. Large groups of sharks sometimes gather together to feed. Such activity can turn into a "feeding frenzy." Sharks may bite wildly at anything and everything within reach—including smaller sharks. In many cases, large sharks also actively hunt their smaller relatives. Juvenile sharks have a tough time reaching adulthood.

5 YEARS

- Joins migratory school
- Hunts spawning fish

CLOSE-UP

Rows of teeth

Shark teeth are arranged in rows. When broken teeth fall out, new ones move forward. Sharks that eat fish or seals have sharp teeth for grabbing and ripping. Those that eat shellfish have flattened teeth for crushing. Whale sharks don't use their 3,000 tiny teeth.

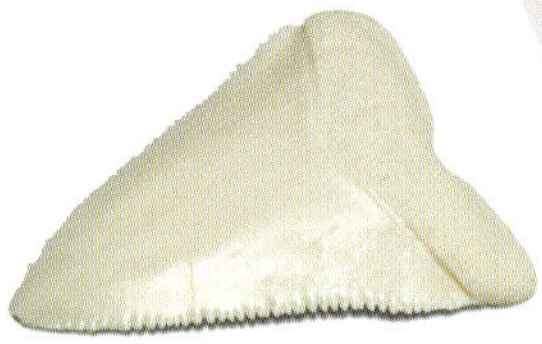

FEATURED FAMILY

Give It a Try

The juvenile hammerhead has left the nursery lagoon and is exploring the rocky seabed and coral reefs of deeper water. As she enters Itabaca Channel, between Santa Cruz and Baltra islands, she comes face to face with a tiger shark. It has come to hunt Galápagos sea lions. Three times bigger than the scalloped hammerhead and much faster, the tiger shark lunges forward. The hammerhead turns sharply and dives, darting under a rock ledge just in time.

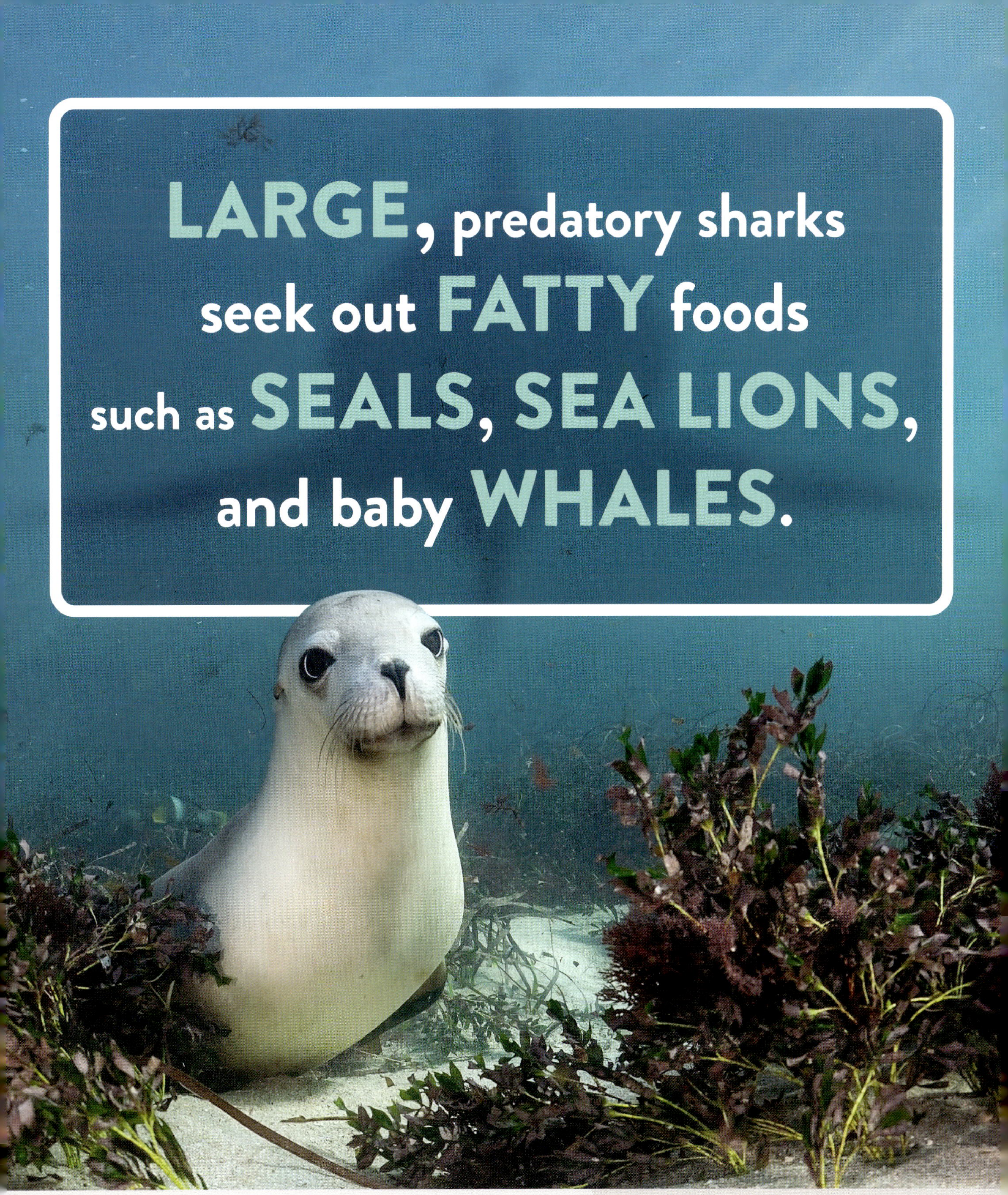

LARGE, predatory sharks seek out FATTY foods such as SEALS, SEA LIONS, and baby WHALES.

6 YEARS

- Travels to Wolf Island cleaning station
- Length: 4.5 feet (1.4 m)

CLOSE-UP

Camouflage

Many sharks are dark on top and light on the bottom. This is called countershading. It makes a shark less detectable from below. Bottom-dwelling sharks are often colored to blend in with their rocky or sandy seafloor habitats.

CHAPTER THREE

LIFE LESSONS

For many sharks, reaching "adulthood" does not necessarily mean they are ready to mate. Female tiger sharks can reproduce as young as 7 or 8 years old, but great whites do not reach maturity until age 30. Greenland sharks must be at least 150 years old before they can give birth! Mating among sharks is dangerous business. Males may bite the females, leaving scars. Sharks sometimes gather at cleaning stations. At these locations, cleaner fish not only eat parasites and dead skin from sharks' bodies, but they also clear out bacteria that could infect wounds. Such a partnership feeds the cleaners and keeps sharks healthy.

10 YEARS

- Returns to Wolf Island annually
- Unconcerned by predators
- Length: 5.3 feet (1.6 m)
- Weight: 114 pounds (51.7 kg)

12.5 YEARS

- Wanders outside Galápagos Marine Reserve
- Hooked by sport fisherman but escapes
- Length: 5.6 feet (1.7 m)

Except when mating and cleaning, most sharks avoid each other. Only a handful of species are social. Sand tiger, sevengill, and blacktip reef sharks have all been known to hunt in small packs like wolves. The 10 hammerhead species have uniquely social lives. Schools of dozens or even hundreds cruise around seamounts and reefs during the day. Then at night, individuals dive to the seabed to hunt. Some sharks stay in roughly the same location their entire lives. Others migrate, or travel seasonally along established routes, usually in pursuit of food sources.

Shark species' life spans vary greatly. Blue sharks usually live 15 to 20 years. Ham-

CLOSE-UP

Hearing

Inner ears help a shark with balance and hearing. Tiny hairs inside the ear pick up vibrations from splashing and low-pitched sounds. Sharks can detect sounds up to 800 feet (244 m) away.

FEATURED FAMILY

This Is How It's Done

At six years old, the scalloped hammerhead is still a juvenile. A tiger or oceanic whitetip shark could make a meal of her. She has joined a school of about 80 scalloped hammerheads and traveled 173 miles (278 km) to Wolf Island. A strong current pushes water over the shark's gills. She drifts at an angle, showing her white belly. It's an invitation. King angelfish and butterflyfish swarm the young hammerhead, gently nibbling away parasites from her skin. She will not harm these cleaners. They provide a valuable service.

Whale sharks live more than 100 YEARS.

15.5 YEARS

- Returns to Santa Cruz lagoon
- Gives birth for the first time
- Length: 7.6 feet (2.3 m)
- Weight: 164 pounds (74.4 kg)

20 YEARS

- Fully grown
- Length: 13.5 feet (4.1 m)
- Weight: 315 pounds (143 kg)

merheads can live twice as long. Dusky and tiger sharks may live up to 50 years, great whites up to 70, and whale sharks more than 100. The longest-lived vertebrate (animal with a backbone) is the Greenland shark. In the icy North Atlantic and Arctic oceans, it can live more than 300 years, scavenging dead seals, whales, and polar bears. Life span is likely related to activity. Blue sharks are highly active, whereas whale sharks move slowly. Greenland sharks barely move at all. Regardless of species, very few shark pups survive to old age.

CLOSE-UP

Overwhelming smells

Below the snout are two nares, or nasal cavities. Inside these are tissues called olfactory lamellae, which capture scents. About two-thirds of a shark's brain is dedicated to identifying smells.

FEATURED FAMILY

Practice Makes Perfect

After cruising around the reef with her school, the young hammerhead breaks away from her companions. It is time to hunt. Her powerful senses enable her to find prey up to three miles (4.8 km) away, but she smells a closer meal tonight. On the ocean floor, nearly 600 feet (183 m) down, she locates an injured diamond stingray. In total darkness, she uses her cephalofoil to pin the stingray. It raises the barb on its tail to stab her. But she doesn't give up. She will have her meal.

28 YEARS

- Gives birth for the last time
- Has birthed nearly 300 pups in her lifetime

30 YEARS

- End of life

CHAPTER FOUR

SHARK SPOTTING

Humans have eaten fish for thousands of years. In recent decades, the demand for seafood has increased dramatically. The fishing industry has responded by removing excessive amounts of fish—including sharks—from the world's oceans. Despite scientists' warnings that many shark species are **endangered**, overfishing has continued. Populations have plummeted—some by as much as 99 percent. From fierce great whites and hammerheads to timid angel and whale sharks, hundreds of species are at risk of disappearing from Earth forever.

A first step toward protecting sharks is to better understand them. Sharks are studied around the world. In Costa Rica and the Galápagos Islands, researchers capture scalloped hammerhead pups. Identification tags are clipped to their dorsal fins, and devices that use **Global Positioning System** (GPS) technology may also be implanted. Such devices can function for several years and do not harm the animals. Similar work on other shark species is being done in Australia, South Africa, and the Bahamas. Scientists with the University of Miami

Shark Research and Conservation Program study a variety of sharks that inhabit Florida's waters.

In 2015, the Georgia Aquarium, Conservation International, and the Indonesian government joined together for a major project—the first of its kind—to study whale sharks. In West Papua's Cenderawasih Bay, researchers got into the water with the massive animals. They measured the sharks, collected blood samples, and attached GPS devices to the gentle giants' fins. The naturally curious whale sharks calmly complied with the testing in exchange for snacks of small fish. The main goal of shark research is to learn what the fish need in order to reproduce and remain healthy in various habitats. That way, suitably protective policies can be enacted.

Public education is also important for shark conservation. Large sharks have a reputation for being dangerous predators. But current studies of great white and tiger sharks, in particular, have revealed them to be intelligent, curious animals with no interest in eating humans. Scientists once studied predatory sharks from the safety of metal cages, but now many shark experts fearlessly free dive with these enormous fish. Perhaps if fear and misunderstanding can be minimized, people will come to recognize the value of conserving sharks for future generations.

FAMILY ALBUM

SNAPSHOTS

The **Halmahera epaulette, or walking, shark** uses its pectoral fins to "walk" along the ocean floor.

The **pyjama shark** dwells on rocky seafloors and in caves off South Africa's coast. It grows to be less than three feet (0.9 m) long.

Roughly the size of a school bus, the **whale shark** is the world's largest fish. It eats tiny fish, **crustaceans**, fish eggs, and floating plants and algae.

Bull sharks can travel into **brackish** water. They have even been spotted swimming 700 miles (1,127 km) up the Mississippi River.

The 24-inch-long (61 cm) **brown shyshark** of coastal South Africa is named for its defensive behavior of curling up in a ball with its tail over its eyes.

To nab prey, the **spinner shark** drives through a school of fish, often making a spinning leap out of the water. These sharks can be more than six feet (1.8 m) long.

The **shortfin mako** is the world's fastest shark. Averaging 10 feet (3 m) long, it can swim for short bursts of up to 60 miles (96.6 km) per hour.

The 12 **wobbegong** species, bottom-dwelling carpet sharks, get their name from an Australian Aboriginal word for "shaggy beard."

The **common thresher shark** can grow 20 feet (6.1 m) long, with its tail accounting for half that length. It stuns prey with a whack of its tail.

Less than eight inches (20.3 cm) long, the smallest known shark species is the **dwarf lantern shark**. It is found only off the coast of Colombia and Venezuela.

Probably the best-known shark is the **great white shark**. It can grow to 21 feet (6.4 m) in length and can weigh 5,000 pounds (2,268 kg).

The **goblin shark** lives deep in the ocean and hunts in total darkness. Its jaws shoot forward and snap shut on prey with lightning speed.

Only four shark species, including the **Ganges shark**, are true freshwater river-dwellers. All river shark species are critically endangered.

WORDS to Know

brackish containing a mixture of salt and fresh water

cartilage firm, flexible body tissue that weighs about half as much as bone

crustaceans animals with no backbone that have a shell covering a soft body

endangered at risk of dying out completely

Global Positioning System a system of electronic devices that work together to determine the location of objects or things that carry a trackable device

parasites animals or plants that live on or inside another living thing (called a host) while giving nothing back to the host; some parasites cause disease or even death

species a group of living beings with shared characteristics and the ability to reproduce with one another

umbilical cord a flexible, tubelike structure through which a female provides an unborn baby with food and oxygen and collects its waste

LEARN MORE

Books

Hubbard, Ben. *Sharks: Get Up Close to Nature's Fiercest Predators*. London: Carlton Kids, 2016.

Nagelhout, Ryan. *Diving with Sharks*. New York: Gareth Stevens, 2014.

Skerry, Brian. *The Ultimate Book of Sharks*. Washington, D.C.: National Geographic, 2018.

Websites

Bester, Cathleen. "Scalloped Hammerhead." Florida Museum of Natural History. https://www.floridamuseum.ufl.edu/discover-fish/species-profiles/sphyrna-lewini/.

Edmonds, Molly. "Shark Facts vs. Shark Myths." World Wildlife Fund. https://www.worldwildlife.org/stories/shark-facts-vs-shark-myths.

"Sharks." Smithsonian Ocean. https://ocean.si.edu/ocean-life/sharks-rays/sharks.

Documentaries

Lucas, Thomas. *Galápagos: Realm of Giant Sharks*. LFBG Galapagos, 2012.

Mauro, Danny. *Shark Divers*. Sport Diver TV, 2017.

Morris, Steve. *Great White Shark: Beyond the Cage of Fear*. Cageless Productions, 2013.

Note: Every effort has been made to ensure that any websites listed above were active at the time of publication. However, because of the nature of the Internet, it is impossible to guarantee that these sites will remain active indefinitely or that their contents will not be altered.

Visit

AQUARIUM OF THE PACIFIC

At Shark Lagoon, visitors can touch some of the sharks.

100 Aquarium Way
Long Beach, CA 90802

GEORGIA AQUARIUM

The only aquarium outside Asia to house whale sharks.

225 Baker Street Northwest
Atlanta, GA 30313

NEW ENGLAND AQUARIUM

Hands-on exhibits feature a variety of small shark species.

1 Central Wharf
Boston, MA 02110

VANCOUVER AQUARIUM

The daily Shark Talk highlights blacktip reef sharks.

845 Avison Way
Vancouver, BC V6G 3E2
Canada

INDEX